P9-BZO-677

Lucky

Lucky

By Jane E. Gerver

Illustrated by Jacqueline Rogers

SCHOLASTIC INC.

New York   Toronto   London   Auckland   Sydney
Mexico City   New Delhi   Hong Kong   Buenos Aires

For Leslie
–J.E.G.

To my models and dear friends,
Kaleigh and Francis, with lots of love.
–J.R.

No part of this publication may be reproduced, or stored in a retrieval system, or transmitted in any form or by any means, electronic, mechanical, photocopying, recording, or otherwise, without written permission of the publisher. For information regarding permissions, write to Scholastic Inc., Attention: Permissions Department, 557 Broadway, New York, NY 10012.

Library of Congress Cataloging-in-Publication Data
Gerver, Jane E.
Lucky / by Jane E. Gerver ; illustrated by Jacqueline Rogers.
p. cm. -- (Breyer stablemates) "Cartwheel books."
Summary: Spurred on by her older sister, Amy works hard to overcome her nervousness so that she and her horse Lucky can compete in their first horse show.
ISBN 0-439-72234-9 (hardcover)
[1. Horses--Fiction. 2. Horse shows--Fiction. 3. Sisters--Fiction.]
I. Rogers, Jacqueline, ill. II. Title.
PZ7.G3264Lu 2007   [E]--dc22   2006019881
ISBN-13: 978-0-439-72234-6
ISBN-10: 0-439-72234-9

Copyright © 2007 by Reeves International, Inc.
All rights reserved. Published by Scholastic Inc.
BREYER, STABLEMATES, and BREYER logos are trademarks and/or registered trademarks of Reeves International, Inc.
SCHOLASTIC, CARTWHEEL BOOKS, and associated logos are trademarks and/or registered trademarks of Scholastic Inc.

10 9 8 7 6 5 4 3 2   07 08 09 10 11

Printed in China
First printing, July 2007

Table of Contents

The Horse Show

Amy and Michele were sisters. Michele was older. Amy was younger. Michele liked green. Amy liked blue. Michele liked french fries. Amy liked mashed potatoes. But there was one thing both sisters loved: horses!

Michele had been riding for many years. She rode hunt seat equitation. And she took lessons at Windy Gate Farm. Her horse's name was Jack.

One day, Michele and her trainer, Paula, were in the tack room. "Michele, you should enter this show," Paula said. "It's next month."

"Oh, I will!" Michele said excitedly. "I haven't missed any shows!"

But Amy had missed *every* show. She had been riding her horse, Lucky, for only one year. And she had just started jumping. She wasn't even sure she liked it, so she stopped taking lessons.

"I love to ride you," she told Lucky. "But I get nervous in front of people. Especially people I don't know!"

Lucky nickered softly in reply.

That evening at dinner, Michele said,
"Amy, did you know there's a horse show in
six weeks? I'm going to be in it!"

"Not me," Amy said.

"But I think the beginner class would be
perfect for you," Michele said.

"No," Amy said.

But the next day, Amy saw the poster about the horse show. There was a sign-up sheet next to it . . . and her name was on it!

"Michele, why did you sign me up?" Amy asked later that day. "I'm too nervous to be in a show! And I'm not good enough." Amy hid her face in Lucky's mane.

"You *can* do it!" her sister said. "I'll help you. And Lucky will help you, too. He knows his stuff."

Chapter 2

Try, Try Again

That night, Amy peeked in Michele's room. The wall was covered with the ribbons and awards Michele had won at her horse shows.

Amy wanted lots of ribbons on her bedroom wall, too.

"I'm going to try," Amy said to herself. "Maybe I *can* do it!"

So after school that week, and on the weekend, Michele and Amy went to the stable. Amy went through what she had learned in her lessons.

First Amy practiced walking, turning, and trotting.

Then she practiced cantering, galloping, and stopping.

"Great job, Amy!" said Michele.

Then Amy practiced jumping. First
Lucky trotted over poles laid on the ground.
He liked that.

"Good boy!" she said. Lucky whinnied
happily.

But when Lucky and Amy got to the fences, something always went wrong.

The first time, Lucky stopped. Amy got too close to the fence and there wasn't enough room for him to jump.

"I'm sorry, boy," Amy said, patting him gently. "Let's try it again."

The second time, Amy got scared right before a jump. She pulled back on the reins, so Lucky stopped. Amy walked Lucky in a circle until she was ready to jump again.

The third time, Amy got too close to the fence again. Lucky did jump, but Amy nearly fell off.

Finally, Lucky jumped the fence just right. But Amy lost her stirrup and slid off sideways. She landed in the dirt. "Ouch!" she cried. Lucky gently nudged Amy with his nose, trying to comfort his friend.

Michele was watching nearby. "You can do it!" she called to her little sister. "Try, try again."

But Amy had had enough. "Forget it!" she said. "I'm never going to be as good as *you*!"

Michele helped her little sister up and brushed the dirt off her.

"When I was your age," Michele said, "I wasn't a good rider. I made lots of mistakes and fell off a few times, too. It takes practice to get better. And you need to learn to trust Lucky more. He knows what he's doing. Let him show you."

But Amy didn't feel any better.

Chapter

3

A New Plan

That evening, Amy went into Michele's bedroom. Amy pointed to all the ribbons and awards.

"How can you say you weren't good?" Amy said. "You have so many ribbons!" She couldn't believe that her sister wasn't always a star.

Michele laughed. "You only see the ribbons I got for winning. You don't see all the times I made mistakes and lost. But I practiced and practiced and got better. I have an idea. Tomorrow, let's ask Mom if my trainer can help you!"

Before falling asleep that night, Amy
thought about what Michele had told her.
"I'm going to keep trying," Amy said.

The next day, Michele saw Paula.
"Would you give Amy lessons to help her
get ready for the horse show?"

"Sure!" said Paula. "I already spoke to
your mother about it. Amy, we'll have you
jumping in no time!" she said.

Soon Amy was busy riding and
listening to Paula's directions — on that
day and each day after that.

The weeks went by and Amy got much better. Soon she and Lucky could jump an entire course of jumps! *I* can *do it!* she thought.

"You're doing great, Amy," Paula said. Amy felt happy. Lucky was happy, too.

"Thank you, Paula," Amy said. "You've helped me so much!"

The day before the show, Amy
carefully bathed and groomed Lucky.

Then Amy cleaned her tack. Michelle
braided Lucky's mane and tail.

And she double-checked her riding
clothes, hat, and boots to make sure they
were spotless.

"I'm nervous," she told Lucky. "But I
think I *can* do this."

It's Showtime!

The next morning, Amy and Michele arrived at the show early. The horses from Windy Gate Farm traveled there in big horse vans.

Amy entered a children's hunt seat equitation over fences class. In this class, Amy would be judged on how well she rode Lucky. Before her class began, she studied the course so she could learn it.

Now it was time for Amy's class to begin. Paula and Michele stood with her in the in-gate.

"Do you know the course, Amy?" asked Paula. Amy nodded.

"Then go on in," said Paula.

"Ready, Lucky?" Amy clucked to her horse.

Amy and Lucky trotted into the ring, picked up a canter, and rode around the course.

Amy made sure to sit properly and keep her head up and eyes forward each time she jumped.

And she tried not to think about the crowd watching her.

As they jumped the last fence, there was a whoop from Paula and Michele. Amy and Lucky had done it! A beautiful round!

"We did it, Lucky!" said Amy. Lucky whinnied happily.

"My first win!" Amy said proudly.

"Thank you, Lucky!"

"I knew you could do it!" Michele said.

"And I know just the place for your ribbon."

"Here's to many more awards!" Michele said after they got home. She put the ribbon above Amy's desk.

"This will always remind you that today was *your* 'Lucky' day!" Michele said.

And Michele hugged her happy little sister.

About the Horses

Facts about Thoroughbreds:

1. Thoroughbreds are originally from England.

2. Thoroughbreds have big lungs and strong legs that allow them to run very fast.

3. Thoroughbreds are used for racing, jumping, eventing, and polo.

4. The average Thoroughbred is about 16 hands tall. A hand is four inches high.

Jerry Irwin / Photo Researchers, Inc

Elisabeth Weiland / Photo Researchers, Inc

Facts about Warmbloods:

1. Dutch Warmbloods are eager, reliable, and intelligent.

2. Dutch Warmbloods are used for dressage, show jumping, eventing, and combined driving.

3. Warmbloods are about 16 hands high.

4. Warmblood colors are chestnut, bay, black, or gray, with white markings often on the face and legs.

When Horses Are All You Dream About...

It has to be Breyer® model horses!

Breyer® model horses are fun to play with and collect!
Meet horse heroes that you know and love. Learn about horses
from foreign lands. Enjoy crafts and games.
Visit us at **www.breyerhorses.com**
for horse fun that never ends!

© 2006 Reeves International, Inc.